BABYMOUSE AN

BABYMOUSE

WILSON

BEST FRIEND!

GEORGIE

PESKY BROTHER!

SQUEAK

TALLEST FRIEND!

FELICIA

BURP!

EATS HOMEWORK!

MEAN GIRL!

LOCKER

*. . . OR ENEMIES!

THEY MAKE
GREAT BEDTIME
STORIES!

BE SURE TO READ **ALL THE BABYMOUSE** BOOKS:

#1 BABYMOUSE: Queen of the World!
#2 BABYMOUSE: Our Hero
#3 BABYMOUSE: Beach Babe
#4 BABYMOUSE: Rock Star
#5 BABYMOUSE: Heartbreaker
#6 CAMP BABYMOUSE
#7 BABYMOUSE: Skater Girl
#8 BABYMOUSE: Puppy Love
#9 BABYMOUSE: Monster Mash
#10 BABYMOUSE: The Musical
#11 BABYMOUSE: Dragonslayer
#12 BABYMOUSE: Burns Rubber
#13 BABYMOUSE: Cupcake Tycoon
#14 BABYMOUSE: Mad Scientist
#15 A Very BABYMOUSE Christmas
#16 BABYMOUSE for President
#17 Extreme BABYMOUSE
#18 Happy Birthday, BABYMOUSE
#19 BABYMOUSE: Bad Babysitter

SHE'D BE NO TROUBLE TO BABYSIT!
FOR ISA

Nursery Rhyme Classics
~PRESENTS~

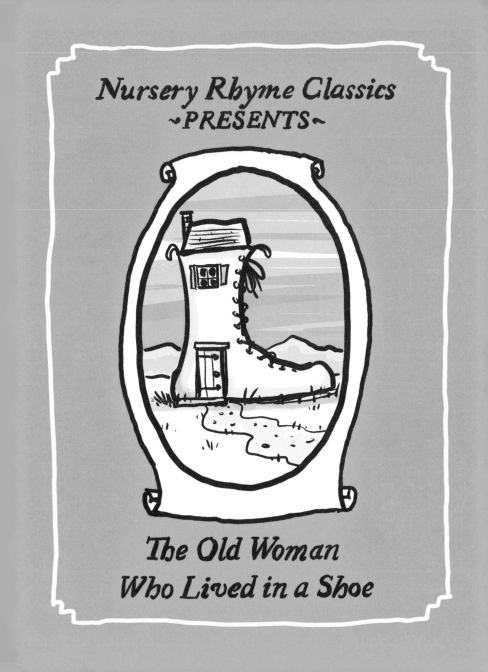

The Old Woman Who Lived in a Shoe

THERE WAS AN OLD WOMAN . . .
WHO LIVED IN A SHOE.
IT'S NOT A SHOE. IT'S A BEDROOM SLIPPER!
SORRY.

THERE WAS AN OLD WOMAN WHO LIVED IN A BEDROOM SLIPPER.
SHE HAD SO MANY CHILDREN . . .
HOP!
WHIRL!
THEY'RE NOT CHILDREN. THEY'RE TROUBLESOME GNOMES.
WE'RE NO TROUBLE AT ALL!
RIGHT. MY BAD.

THERE WAS AN OLD WOMAN WHO LIVED IN A BEDROOM SLIPPER. SHE HAD SO MANY TROUBLESOME GNOMES, SHE DIDN'T KNOW WHAT TO DO.

AND MAY I JUST SAY THAT YOU ARE TAKING SOME SERIOUS LIBERTIES WITH THE ORIGINAL TEXT?

THIS IS MY RHYME, BUDDY!

OF COURSE. OF COURSE.

UGH! WHAT IS THAT SMELL?
SNIFF!
SNIFF!
BABYMOUSE!
BLINK!
STINKY SLIPPER, BABYMOUSE! STINKY SLIPPER!
SO YOU'RE READING A COMIC?
WHAT? GIRLS READ COMICS, TOO, YOU KNOW.
COMICS SQUAD

THE SOOPER SCOOTER!

IT SCOOTS!

IT FLIES!

IT DOES SOMERSAULTS!

IT HAS A MILK SHAKE MACHINE!

IT'S THE SOOPER SCOOTER!

$79.95

ZOOM!

MOM! MOM! CAN I BUY THIS?

$79.95? THAT'S A LOT OF MONEY, BABYMOUSE.
DO YOU HAVE ANY ALLOWANCE LEFT?

UHH . . .

TWO DAYS EARLIER.

CUPCAKE PARLOR

OPEN

CUPCAKE PARLOR

CLOSED

LUNCH.

HMM . . .

SORRY, BABYMOUSE. THAT SEAT IS TAKEN.
YOU CAN'T SIT HERE.
TOTALLY TAKEN.

HA! HA!
HA!
HA! HA!
HA!
OVER HERE, BABYMOUSE!

I SAVED A SEAT FOR YOU!

THANKS, WILSON!
GRIN!

BABYMOUSE, I WAS SUPPOSED TO BABYSIT THIS SATURDAY NIGHT. BUT I HAVE TO GO SEE MY GRANDPARENTS.

WOULD YOU BE INTERESTED IN BABYSITTING?

BABYSIT?

TAP!

I'M YOUR NEW NANNY.
BABYPOPPINS.
THE NANNY HAS MESSY WHISKERS!
YANK!
HEY!
BLINK!

SO WHAT DO YOU THINK, BABYMOUSE?
IT'S A FUN WAY TO MAKE EXTRA MONEY.
YOU GET PAID?!?
OF COURSE.
ZOOM!

I'LL DO IT!

GREAT!
I'LL TELL THE MOM.

REAL BABIES, BABYMOUSE?
DO YOU REMEMBER WHAT HAPPENED WHEN YOU BROUGHT THE CLASS PET HOME AND YOU WERE SUPPOSED TO WATCH IT?

DO NOT OVERFEED!

SHAKE!
SHAKE!

FISH FOOD

FISH FOOD

YOU LOOK HUNGRY. I'LL FEED YOU A CUPCAKE.
FISH FOOD

FISH FOOD

SPLOOSH!
DO NOT OVERFEED

LATER.

I DON'T THINK YOU CAN OVERFEED BABIES.
CAN YOU?
SIGH.

LATER.

ROCK-A-BYE, BABY . . .

ROCK-A-BYE,

BABYMOUSE,
YAWN!

IN THE LOCKER-TOP.
ROCK ROCK

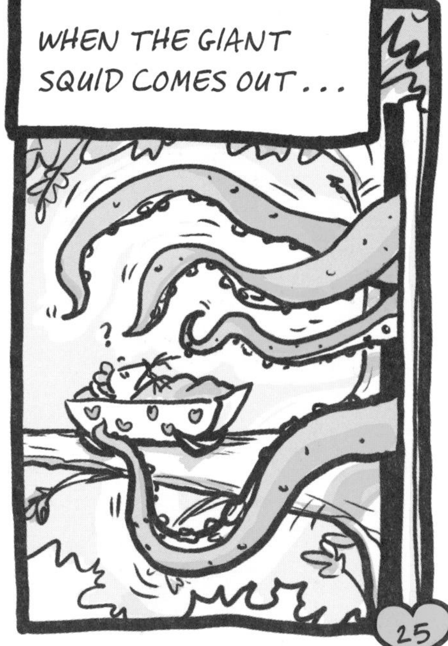
WHEN THE GIANT SQUID COMES OUT . . .
?

THE CRADLE WILL—
SHAKE SHAKE

FALL.
FLIP!
(I CAN'T BEAR TO WATCH.)

WHAT KIND OF LULLABY IS THIS, ANYWAY?
ZOOM!

RIIINNNGGG!!!

WHUNK!

SO YOU WERE IN A CRADLE IN A TREE IN YOUR LOCKER AND A GIANT SQUID SHOOK IT AND THAT'S WHY YOU'RE LATE FOR CLASS AGAIN?
OMEWORK IS FUN!
THAT LULLABY ALWAYS SEEMED KIND OF DANGEROUS TO ME.
OUCH. STUPID LULLABY.
PRINCIPAL'S OFFICE

SATURDAY NIGHT.
RINNG!
HI, BABYMOUSE!
HI, MRS. LADYBUG!

I ALREADY PUT HIM TO BED.
THERE ARE BOTTLES IN THE FRIDGE IN CASE HE WAKES UP.
OKAY!
ZZZZZ . . .
BUT HE'S A PRETTY EASY BABY. HE'LL PROBABLY SLEEP THE WHOLE TIME WE'RE GONE.
CALL US IF YOU NEED ANYTHING AT ALL. AND HELP YOURSELF TO THE SNACKS.
HAVE FUN!

LATER.
WAAAAAAHHH!

WAAAHH!!
MUNCH
MUNCH
DONUTS

WAAAHHHH!!!
MUNCH
MUNCH
ROCK

WAAAAAHHHHH!!!

WAAAAHHHHHHHHHHHHHHHHH
WAAAHHHH!!
WAAAAAAHHHHHH HHHHHHHH

WAAAAHHHHHHHHH!!

UH, I WONDER WHY HE'S CRYING.

DONUTS

FEED THE BABY!

FEED THE BABY!

FEED THE BABY, RODENT CREATURE!

BEE-ZORT!

I GUESS HE WAS JUST HUNGRY.
DONUTS
EXCELLENT GUESS, BABYMOUSE.

LATER.
SLURP
SLURP
WOW. THAT IS ONE HUNGRY BABY.
SLURP
SLURP
CHOMP!
CHOMP!

THE VERY HUNGRY BABYMOUSE

ATE SOME CUPCAKES.

AND ATE SOME MORE CUPCAKES.

AND SOME MORE.

SLURP
PAUSE
SLURP
?

WHY DID HE STOP EATING?
POP!

IS HE FINALLY FULL?

BURRRPPP!!

HAVE YOU HEARD OF BURPING A BABY, BABYMOUSE?
NOW YOU TELL ME.
UGH.

A LITTLE LATER.

THERE. YOU'RE ALL CLEAN AND FRESH NOW.

LAUNDRY

EWW . . .

HMM . . .
DISPOSABLE DIAPERS

SOON.
WET WIPEZ

UH, BABYMOUSE. I THINK THE DIAPER'S SUPPOSED TO GO ON THE BABY.

YOU TRY SMELLING THIS, BUSTER.
FWIP!
WET

A LITTLE LATER.
ZZZ . . .
ROCK
ROCK

GET PLENTY OF SLEEP
ZZZ . . .

ZZZ . . .

ZZZ . . .

WAAAHH!

WAAAHH!!!

ZZZ . . .
ROCK
ROCK

ZZZ . . .

WAAAHH!!

ZZZ . . .

TWO HOURS LATER.
TIP TOE
TIP TOE

MONSTER MOVIE MARATHON
PRESENTS:
WHEN ZOMBIES ATTACK!

MUNCH
MUNCH
PRICELESS VASE

AAAGH!
BRAINS!!

YEAH, I'M BABYSITTING. THE BABY'S ASLEEP.
BLAH
BLAH
BLAH
WANT TO GO TO THE SOCK HOP NEXT WEEK?
BANG BANG!
HANG ON. SOMEONE'S AT THE DOOR.
BANG! BANG!

PANT
PANT
?

THE ZOMBIES ARE COMING!

ZOMBIES?
SLAM!

CRASH!
GASP!

SLAM!
GASP!
WE WANT TO EAT YOUR CUPCAKES!

FLING!

GASP!

SMASH!

MY HEIRLOOM VASE!
SORRY ABOUT THAT!
BUT AT LEAST THE BABY'S ASLEEP!
WAAAAAAH!!!
WINCE!

A FEW DAYS LATER.

BEEP!
BEEP!
BEEP!

YEP! MY BROTHER'S A TODDLER.
?
WONDERFUL! SEE YOU SATURDAY NIGHT.

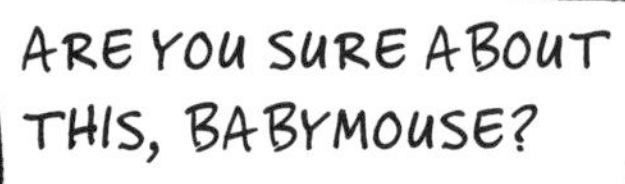
ARE YOU SURE ABOUT THIS, BABYMOUSE?

I WANT A SOOPER SCOOTER!

BESIDES— TODDLERS ARE SO MUCH EASIER THAN BABIES.
NO BOTTLE OR DIAPERS.
VROOM!
IF YOU SAY SO.

SATURDAY NIGHT.
AND THERE ARE THE CHILDREN.
OH, THEY'RE SO CUTE!
HERE'S A LIST SHOWING THEIR NIGHTLY ROUTINE.
THE LIST
• BATH
• BOOK
• CLEAN!!!

YOU'LL NEED TO GIVE THEM A BATH.

NO PROBLEM!

THEY LIKE A BOOK READ TO THEM BEFORE THEY GO TO SLEEP.
NO PROBLEM!

BUT MOST IMPORTANT, PLEASE MAKE SURE THE HOUSE IS CLEAN WHEN WE GET HOME.
I DON'T LIKE MESSES.
NO PROBLEM! HAVE A GREAT NIGHT.

CLICK!
MOMMY!
MOMMY!
MOMMY!
WAH!
WAH!
LOOKS LIKE YOU HAVE A LITTLE **PROBLEM** THERE, BABYMOUSE.
OR MAYBE THREE OF THEM.
WAAAHHH!
AAAHH!
WAAAAAH!

HEY, GUYS! WANT TO DO SOMETHING FUN?
WAAAAAHH!!

?
?
?

UH . . . WE COULD . . .

ER . . .
UM . . .
BOOKS
SHUFFLE
PAPER

HOW ABOUT WE DO FINGER PAINTING?!

YAYYYY!!!!!!!
OOP! OOP!
CLAP CLAP

A LITTLE LATER.

BLURP

BLAT

SPLAT

ARE YOU SURE ABOUT THIS, BABYMOUSE?
I HAVE TO GIVE THEM A BATH ANYWAY.
SHRUG

POTTY!
POTTY!

COME ON!
LET'S GO!

SOON.

TOY BOX
BLURP!
LOOKS LIKE YOU'LL HAVE TO GIVE THE WALLS A "BATH," TOO, BABYMOUSE.
SLUMP
UGH.

BATH TIME.
SPLISH
DRIP
SPLASH
DRIP
DRIP
DRIP
DRIP
DRIP
DRIP
DRIP
SPLISH
SPLASH
OH DEAR!

IT'S A BLUSTERY DAY!
HUNNY
SPLASH
DRIP
IT CERTAINLY IS A BLUSTERY DAY!
HUNNY

IT ALWAYS RAINS ON ME.

WHAT DO YOU THINK, FELICIA?

THE WONDERFUL THING ABOUT FELICIAS IS THAT I'M THE ONLY ONE!
BOING!
SPLASH!
BOING!

HEY!
HA!
SPLASH!
BLINK!
SPLASH!
SPLASH!
SPLASH!
SPLISH!
SPLASH!
SPLOOSH!
WELL, IT CERTAINLY IS A VERY BLUSTERY DAY, BABYMOUSE.
TYPICAL.
INSIDE, I MEAN.

BEDTIME.

DONE!
BOOK TIME.

FIVE LITTLE MONKEYS JUMPING ON THE BED . . .

THREE LITTLE MONKEYS JUMPING ON THE BED.
BOING
BOING
BOING

ONE FELL DOWN AND BONKED BABYMOUSE'S HEAD.
BONK!
HEY!
BABYMOUSE WAS EXHAUSTED AFTER CLEANING UP FINGER PAINT AND WATER, AND SO SHE SAID . . .
BOING
BOING
BOING
SCRUB SCRUB
NO MORE MONKEYS JUMPING ON THE BED!

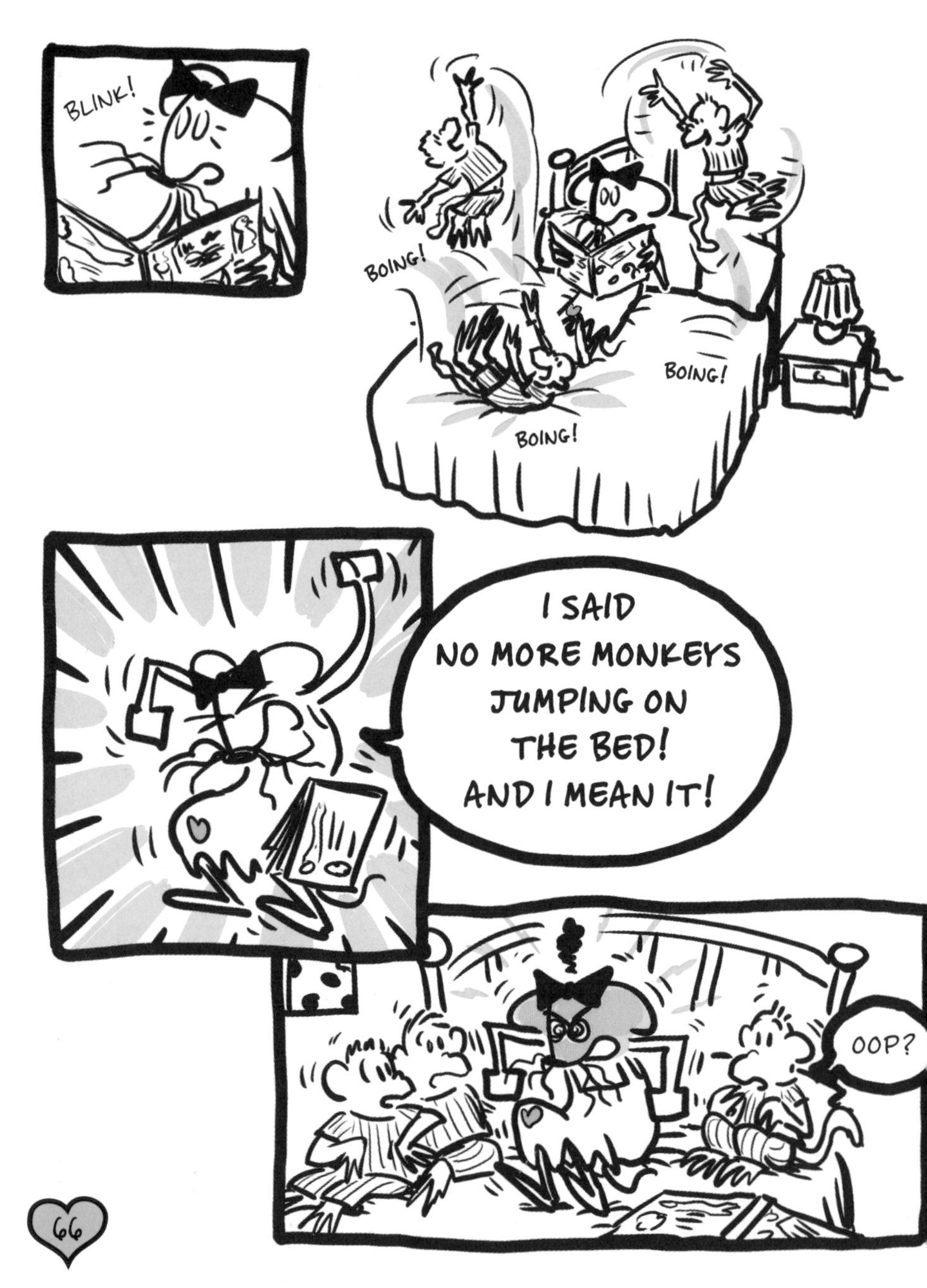
BLINK!
BOING!
BOING!
BOING!
I SAID NO MORE MONKEYS JUMPING ON THE BED! AND I MEAN IT!
OOP?

CLICK!
WHEW.

BOING!
BOING!
BOING!

ZOOM!

I SAID NO MORE JUMPING ON THE BED!

HUH?

BOUNCE! BOUNCE!

BOUNCE!
BOUNCE!
!

BOUNCE!
BOUNCE!
WELL, YOU NEVER SAID ANYTHING ABOUT JUMPING ON THE **ROOF.**
OOF!

THE NEXT DAY AT SCHOOL.
HOW DID IT GO WITH THE MONKEY TRIPLETS?
UH . . .
MY HOUSE!
SORRY ABOUT THAT!
AT LEAST THE ROOF WASN'T DAMAGED FROM THE MONKEYS JUMPING ON IT.

CRACK!

NOT SO GOOD.
I THINK I'M A BAD BABYSITTER.

TODDLERS CAN BE HARD.

I KNOW THIS MOM WHO HAS A FIVE-YEAR-OLD WHO NEEDS A BABYSITTER. HE'S A MELLOW LITTLE KID.

WHADDYA SAY, BABYMOUSE?
HEY!
WAIT FOR ME!
ZOOM!
I'LL DO IT!

A FEW DAYS LATER.

HI! I'M BABYMOUSE.
YOUR NEW BABYSITTER.

NOD

OTTO'S A LITTLE SHY.
BUT HE'LL WARM UP.
NOW, I JUST HAVE TO RUN A FEW ERRANDS. SEE YOU IN A BIT.
OKAY!
WHAT DO YOU WANT TO DO, OTTO?
SHRUG

HEY, LOOK! I BROUGHT A BUNCH OF COOL STUFF!

BOARD GAMES!
COMICS!
ROBOTS!

OLD-FASHIONED BICYCLE!
BUCKET O' ANTS!
ALIENS!

AND BIGFOOT!

WHADDYA SAY?
SHRUG
BEE-ZORT. SAD OWL BOY.
SIGH.
SHAKE

A SPOONFUL OF CUPCAKES MAKES LITTLE OWLS HAPPY!

LITTLE OWLS HAPPY!
LITTLE OWLS HAPPY!
A SPOONFUL OF CUPCAKES MAKES LITTLE OWLS HAPPY!
IN A MOST DELIGHTFUL WAY!

SHAKE
SHAKE

I THINK YOU NEED MORE THAN A CUPCAKE TO CHEER THIS LITTLE GUY UP.
SIGH.

THE FOLLOWING WEEK.

THANKS, BABYMOUSE.
YOU'RE WELCOME.

HMM . . .

THE NEXT DAY.
I HAVE A GREAT IDEA, OTTO.
LET'S GO TO THE PLAYGROUND!
NO!
BUT WHY NOT? I SEE YOU LOOKING AT IT ALL THE TIME.

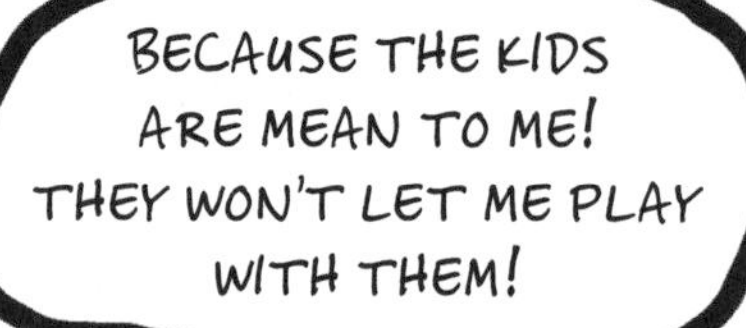

AND I THOUGHT THE TRIPLET MONKEYS WERE HARD.

THE NEXT DAY AT SCHOOL.
HOW'S IT GOING WITH THE LITTLE OWL?
FINE, ACTUALLY. HE'S A GREAT LITTLE KID.
SHOVE!
HEH HEH HEH
APT 9

IT'S JUST THAT HE'S SO SAD. THE OTHER KIDS ARE BEING MEAN TO HIM AT THE PLAYGROUND.
THAT'S HARD.
ALL HE NEEDS IS ONE FRIEND.
COMIX
ONE FRIEND.

THE NEXT DAY.
I DON'T WANT TO GO TO THE PLAYGROUND!
STOMP!
NOBODY WILL PLAY WITH ME!
I'LL PLAY WITH YOU.
COME ON, OTTO! LET'S PLAY CUPCAKE TAG.
WHAT'S CUPCAKE TAG?
SHRUG

CUPCAKE TAG! YOU'RE IT!
TAG! YOU'RE FROSTED!
AHA! RAINBOW SPRINKLES BONUS!
?
ZIP!
HEY! FLYING? NO FAIR!
SWISH
FLAP
FLAP
CHUCKLE.

A LITTLE LATER.
UM, CAN I PLAY, TOO? YOUR GAME SEEMS REALLY FUN.
I DON'T KNOW.
WHAT DO YOU THINK, OTTO?
CAN HE PLAY WITH US?
SURE.
WELL DONE, BABYMOUSE.

END OF THE DAY.
OTTO'S TOTALLY COME OUT OF HIS SHELL. YOU'RE REALLY GOOD WITH KIDS, BABYMOUSE.
YOU'RE A NATURAL BABYSITTER.
BABYMOUSE!
SWOOSH!
I LOVE YOU, BABYMOUSE!
YOU'RE THE BEST BABYSITTER EVER!!

A FEW MONTHS LATER.
BOFFO'S TOY EMPORIUM!
TOYS!
YOWZA!
PUTT
PUTT
PUTT
WAIT—IT CAN'T ACTUALLY FLY?
IS IT EVERY BIT AS AMAZING AS YOU IMAGINED, BABYMOUSE?
IT'S EVEN BETTER!
ZIP!
WHY, BABYMOUSE?
BECAUSE I EARNED IT.
YOU CERTAINLY DID, BABYMOUSE.

BABYMOUSE'S BABYSITTING TIPS

BE CHEERFUL!

ENCOURAGE GOOD HYGIENE!

HELP WITH HOMEWORK!

PREPARE YOUR CHARGES A HEALTHY DINNER!

ABOVE ALL, SAFETY FIRST!

YOU DRAW IT!

CHARACTER: GEORGIE

1.

2.

3.

4.

READ ABOUT *SQUISH'S AMAZING ADVENTURES* IN:

#1 SQUISH: Super Amoeba

#2 SQUISH: Brave New Pond

#3 SQUISH: The Power of the Parasite

#4 SQUISH: Captain Disaster

#5 SQUISH: Game On!

#6 SQUISH: Fear the Amoeba

If you like Babymouse,
you'll love these other great books
by Jennifer L. Holm!

THE BOSTON JANE TRILOGY
EIGHTH GRADE IS MAKING ME SICK
THE FOURTEENTH GOLDFISH
MIDDLE SCHOOL IS WORSE THAN MEATLOAF
OUR ONLY MAY AMELIA
PENNY FROM HEAVEN
TURTLE IN PARADISE